The Gingerbread Man

KANDACE CHIMBIRI

ILLUSTRATED BY RICHY SÁNCHEZ AYALA

BLOOMSBURY EDUCATION

Bloomsbury Publishing Plc

50 Bedford Square, London, WC1B 3DP, UK

29 Earlsfort Terrace, Dublin 2, Ireland

BLOOMSBURY, BLOOMSBURY EDUCATION and the Diana logo
are trademarks of Bloomsbury Publishing Plc

First published in Great Britain in 2021 by Bloomsbury Publishing Plc

A catalogue record for this book is available from the British Library

ISBN: PB: 978-1-4729-8896-6; ePDF: 978-1-4729-8897-3; ePub: 978-1-4729-8899-7;
enhanced ePub: 978-1-4729-8898-0

2 4 6 8 10 9 7 5 3 1

Printed and bound in China by Leo Paper Products, Heshan, Guangdong

All papers used by Bloomsbury Publishing Plc are natural, recyclable products from wood
grown in well managed forests and other sources. The manufacturing processes conform to the
environmental regulations of the country of origin

To find out more about our authors and books visit www.bloomsbury.com
and sign up for our newsletters

Chapter One

Once upon a time an old man and an old woman lived together in a small wooden house. In front of their house they had the most beautiful garden. Everyone in the village admired the colourful flowers.

In the back yard the old couple had enough room for their cow to sleep at night.

Although the old couple were mostly happy, sometimes they felt sad because they wanted to have children but they didn't have any.

One night the old woman had a dream. Her ancestors appeared to her and said, "Bake a little boy of ginger and you and your husband will be very happy."

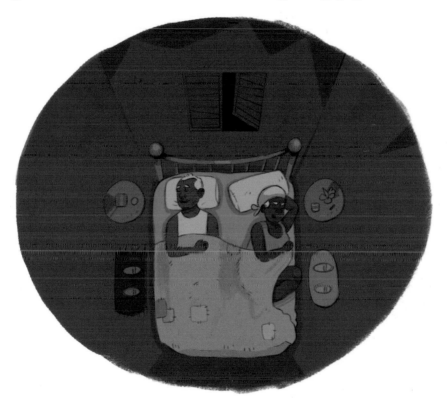

The next morning, while the old man went to milk and then tie out the cow, the old woman started to bake.

She made a ginger dough mix.
Then she rolled most of the dough out
flat and cut it into a little man with a
head, neck, body, arms and legs.
For his eyes she used raisins.

Then she shaped the rest of the dough into his nose and pressed it into his face. Finally, she took two whole almonds to make his wonderful wide smiling mouth.

When the oven was nice and hot, the old woman put her creation in to bake. Soon the dough was baked to a beautiful deep dark brown colour and smelling lovely. The old woman opened the oven to take a peek...

But before she could say a word the gingerbread man jumped out of the tray and out of the window.

Chapter Two

"Stop! Stop!" shouted the old lady, running after the gingerbread man. But the gingerbread man ran away from her, laughing:

"Run, run as fast as you can! You can't catch me, I'm the gingerbread man!"

The old woman chased after the gingerbread man but she couldn't catch him.
The gingerbread man ran past the old man who had just finished tying out the cow.

"Help!" cried the old lady. "Our little gingerbread man is running away."

"Stop! Stop!" shouted the old man. But the gingerbread man laughed at him, too:

"Run, run as fast as you can! You can't catch me, I'm the gingerbread man!" The old woman and the old man chased after the gingerbread man but they couldn't catch him.

Chapter Three

The gingerbread man ran through the
village shop and into the yard behind.
The chickens crowed, "Stop! You smell
delicious. We want to eat you!"

But the gingerbread man laughed:
"Run, run as fast as you can! You can't catch me, I'm the gingerbread man!"
The old woman, the old man and the chickens chased after the gingerbread man but they couldn't catch him.

The gingerbread man ran past the big farm. The horse shouted, "Stop! You smell delicious. I want to eat you!"

But the gingerbread man laughed
even louder:
"Run, run as fast as you can! You can't
catch me, I'm the gingerbread man!"

The old woman, the old man, the chickens and the horse chased after the gingerbread man but they couldn't catch him.

Then the gingerbread man ran past the big house. The dog barked, "Stop! You smell delicious. I want to eat you!" But the gingerbread man just ran, laughing harder.

"Run, run as fast as you can! You can't catch me, I'm the gingerbread man!"

The old woman, the old man, the chickens, the horse and the dog all chased after the gingerbread man but they couldn't catch him.

The gingerbread man looked back over his shoulder and did a little dance.

"Ha ha! None of them will ever catch me," he said and off he ran, even faster than before.

Then he came to a river.
"Oh no! They *will* catch me now,"
he said.

Chapter Four

Along came a monkey. The monkey
smiled. "Oh, little gingerbread man,
can't you swim? Let me be your friend.
Get on my tail and I will take you
across the river."

So the gingerbread man climbed onto the monkey's tail and the monkey waded into the water.

The monkey said, "Oh! The water is getting deeper. Get on my shoulders or you'll get wet and float away in little pieces."

The gingerbread man didn't want to get wet and float away in little pieces so he climbed onto the monkey's shoulders.

Then the monkey said, "Oh! The water is getting even deeper. Soon only my head will be above the water. Get on my nose or you'll get wet and float away in little pieces."

The gingerbread man agreed that would be much safer so he climbed onto the monkey's nose.
The monkey smelled the delicious gingery smell of the gingerbread man and smiled to himself.

As soon as he climbed out of the river, the monkey threw back his head and tossed the gingerbread man up in the air. He closed his eyes and opened his mouth…

"Oh dear," sighed the gingerbread man as he clung on to a tree. "Oh dear, oh dear. What good luck that I got caught in these thick branches."

The monkey began to shake the tree. He shook it so hard that the gingerbread man couldn't hold on any longer. But just as the gingerbread man fell from the tree...

A stone hit the monkey on the nose and he ran away in surprise. The old couple didn't want to lose their lovely little gingerbread man.

They had swum across the river together to save him from the monkey. The old woman was an expert with her gutterperk.

The old woman and the old man smiled at the gingerbread man.

The old woman said, "Won't you come and live with us? I'll make you a gingerbread house."

"What a good idea," the gingerbread man thought to himself.

So they walked back together to their small wooden house.

The old man put the gingerbread man on his shoulder when they passed the dog, the horse and the chickens.

And the three of them lived happily ever after.